SOUTHSEA'S
Secret Gardeners
Shelagh Moore

© Shelagh Moore 2021

Published by Moore Associates

978-0-9928029-9-8

Illustrations: Gary Wing

Design: Charles Design Associates

The Journey, Conspiracy on Mars, The Boy Who Helped a King and *Keeping Up with the Greens* are stories that appear in the Reading Units developed for Exam Papers Plus. For more information about Exam Papers Plus go to: www.exampapersplus.co.uk

Other books available to purchase on Amazon in this series

The Journey
Shelagh Moore
978-0-9928029-6-7 £4.99

Conspiracy on Mars
Shelagh Moore
978-0-9928029-4-3 £4.99

The Boy Who Helped a King
Shelagh Moore
978-0-9928029-7-4 £4.99

Keeping up with the Greens
Shelagh Moore £4.99

Chapter One

The twins were a pair of interesting eight-year-olds. Their mum said they were bound to be interesting with a mum who was Irish and a dad from Barbados! Ailis was three minutes older than Aiden and considered herself to be the eldest. Aiden didn't mind; he was quite happy being his parent's only son. The twins' Celtic names were chosen by their parents, Maria and Bastian, because they met in Ireland. The children had been born there, too, in a small town called Abbeyfeale, in County Limerick. Abbeyfeale was surrounded by farms, and the twins had enjoyed walking through the fields with their parents to visit their grandparents' house for tea and cake.

The family had moved to England when the twins were five, as Maria and Bastian had been offered jobs there. They had recently moved into a semi-detached house near the Queen's Hotel in the seaside town of Southsea and had spent a lot of time decorating and modernising their new home. The twins were pleased now that the building, painting and decorating experience was over and they could finally relax in their own bedrooms. They liked living in Southsea and enjoyed their walks on the Common and by the sea, but they sometimes wished there were fields nearby as they remembered their walks in Ireland.

Ailis looked like her mum, with hair that had red or ginger tints that gleamed in the sunshine. Aiden had dark, curly hair like his dad's and deep-brown eyes. They were both tall for their age, and they were called 'Double A' by their friends at school.

Ailis and Aiden knew that some children lived next door, but they had not met them yet; they went to different schools and their garden had very high walls. The twins sometimes talked about this and had not yet worked out how they could get to know them. Ailis and Aiden were friendly children and enjoyed spending time with their school friends. As they said to each other, "School's alright, except for the work!"

The new house was roomy, and the thing the twins liked most about it was the cellar. The cellar was not plastered or furnished; it only had a light and some old boxes in it. It was a space just waiting to be used for something! The twins wanted it to be seen as theirs. They were working on ideas, but had not yet thought of a use for it. That was all about to change!

School was buzzing with the news that there was a new teacher, and he was going to teach horticulture. That sounded like quite a different sort of lesson. The twins were curious, as were their friends: what, they wondered, was horticulture? It turned out that the new teacher was going to work with a chosen class on a project outside on the school field – and the chosen class was theirs! Anything out of the classroom was a big YES for the twins, so they decided they would work hard at horticulture, whatever it was!

"I like the idea of doing something out of class," Ailis told Aiden on the way home.

"We could look up the word horticulture and see what it means," Aiden suggested. "Mum and Dad might stop nagging us about reading if they see us using the dictionary and reference books."

Chapter Two

Ailis and Aiden hurried home and went straight to Aiden's room to use his dictionary to look up the word horticulture. Mum stopped in shock as she passed Aiden's room and saw the twins reading a book together. She was in a hurry so didn't ask what they were reading, but she reported to their dad that night: "I saw Ailis and Aiden in his room today reading a book. Have you any idea what that is about? They must be up to something!"

"Not a clue," responded their dad. "I just hope they keep on reading. It will help their school work and their writing."

Dad was keen for the twins to gain knowledge. He had worked hard to get his qualifications and a good job. He thought that learning was important and wished that the twins were more interested in their schoolwork.

The twins discovered that horticulture was 'the art of cultivating gardens'. They then looked up 'cultivate' and found that it meant 'to prepare and use land for crops or gardening'. They looked at each other and smiled. "We must be planting a school garden!" said Aiden grinning. "That'll keep us out of the classroom!"

"You bet! It'll be hard work, though. It will take a lot of digging, clearing and planting," replied Ailis. "We need to read up about gardening to show the new teacher that we would be good workers and make sure we get picked for his team!"

At the weekend, Dad was surprised to see the twins sitting in Aiden's room and actually reading a gardening book. "They're reading a gardening book," he reported to Mum. "What is going on?"

"Come on. We'll ask them," said Mum.

When they got to Aiden's room, they saw an even stranger sight – the twins were writing!

"What are you doing?" asked Mum curiously.

"Oh, we're just doing some school stuff, Mum," responded Ailis.

"We thought we'd better get on with it to impress the new teacher," Aiden added.

"What does the new teacher teach?" Dad asked.

"Oh, just horticulture," was the reply. The twins' parents were puzzled. Their children liked painting, music and being outside – why the sudden interest in this lesson? The twins had not mentioned the bit about making a school garden, otherwise they would have understood at once. They would be working outside, digging and planting – out of the classroom!

As the twins read, they found out that gardening was an all-year-round job. Each season had special tasks that needed to be done. They learnt that there was a season for preparing the soil, and times for planting, growing, harvesting and clearing the soil to start the whole cycle again. "We're going to be busy," said Aiden. "It looks interesting though, doesn't it? Who'd have thought there was so much to do to make a garden? No wonder Granddad in Ireland is always out in his garden doing something."

"And it's the same in Barbados. We can write to granddad and Tata and tell them what we are hoping to do at school," Ailis stated. "They will be pleased to hear from us and could send us some tips."

Ailis and Aiden each wrote a letter. They asked their dad to send them by email to their grandparents and ask for a quick reply. By this time, their parents were beginning to wonder if they were up to something. Still, they were reading and writing, which was good for their learning. Mum and Dad knew how thrilled the grandparents would be to get letters from Ailis and Aiden, even by email. They were right – when the emails arrived in Ireland and Barbados, there were two surprised and delighted sets of grandparents. They decided to encourage this new interest. They took pictures of their gardens and wrote about the sort of work they did in them. The twins' Irish grandfather seemed to spend a lot of time hoeing and getting rid of weeds, while their grandmother, their Tata, in Barbados sent a picture of an old wheelbarrow in which she had planted herbs, such as camomile for soothing tea, lemongrass, horehound for colds, lemon balm, mint and dandelion. "Herbs," she wrote, "add flavour to meals. Some make good drinks, some make good salads and some help you to get better if you are ill."

The twins went into school on Monday armed with some ideas and an understanding of what horticulture was. They waited, suppressing their excitement, for the lesson on horticulture to begin. Their new teacher walked into the classroom. He was a medium-sized man with rather long red hair, which was tied back with a band. He was dressed in cord trousers and a well-worn woollen jumper. He didn't look like the teachers they were used to seeing in their classroom!

"Good morning, Class. How are you all? Looking forward to learning about our plans for this term, I hope," his voice boomed across the classroom. The pupils looked at each other – what was he going to tell them? "As it's spring, this is the time for...?" he paused and looked around expectantly at the staring faces. Two hands shot up in the air and waved enthusiastically at him, as 8-year-olds do when they know the answer to a question. He raised an enquiring eyebrow. "Well?" he asked, looking at Aiden.

"It's the time to prepare for planting, Sir," replied Aiden, looking pleased with himself.

"Anything to add?" the teacher pointed at Ailis, who still had her hand up.

"We have to dig over the soil, get rid of the weeds and plan out where we want to plant things," she said, looking at the teacher and hoping she had impressed him with her knowledge.

"Well done," was the reply. "You two seem to have a good idea of what we will need to do to create a school garden. However, before we start, we need to learn about soil and plants."

Chapter Three

The class was surprised – what was there to know about soil? They soon found out. Their teacher, who was called Mr Green, explained that you have to know what type of soil you have so that you can plant the right plants. It was obvious when they thought about it! The class put on their outdoor clothes and went outside with Mr Green, taking some small dishes and trowels with them. They were told to work in pairs and get a couple of samples of earth from two different parts of the area that was marked out in the corner of the playing field. The twins decided to work together to make sure they both got on Mr Green's gardening team. They collected their soil samples and waited to be told what to do next.

"Now, put a little bit of water in each dish and stir it into the soil. Not too much water – we don't want a muddy puddle, do we?" boomed Mr Green and laughed. He did have a voice that could easily be heard around the whole field. Ailis put water in one sample and Aiden put water in the other, and they stirred it in. Then they were told to let them dry for a while.

Back in the classroom, Mr Green told the children that there were three main types of soil: sandy soil, clay soil and silty soil. They were all given notebooks and told to write their names on them and open them at the first page. They had to follow the usual routine, which teachers always seem to like: title – 'Types of Soil' – day and date. When this was done, they had to write what they had done so far in no more than six sentences; Mr Green didn't want lots of marking, they thought! They did wonder why teachers always wanted you to write things down in notebooks. They always seemed to have lots of work to mark – couldn't pupils just tell them the answers?

By the time the writing was done, the soil had dried enough for stage two of their experiment. Stage two was good fun! They had to take the soil between their fingers and roll it into a ball, and then they had to note the results in their books. Did the soil break up easily when they pressed it between their fingers? Did it take a bit of time to break apart? Or did it feel sticky and change shape when squeezed? The children all wrote down their results. They had only taken soil samples from the marked out area but, strangely, they got different results.

Mr Green explained that this showed there were three different types of soil in the area where the garden would be. The soil that broke apart easily and felt gritty was sandy soil. The soil that felt smoother and took longer to break apart was silty soil. Finally, the soil that was sticky and could be pressed into different shapes was clay soil. They now knew the types of soil they had to work with and could learn more about how to prepare it for planting. The children thought this was quite interesting and were sorry when the lesson ended. Then came the dreaded 'h' word – homework! It actually wasn't too bad, as far as homework went. They had to repeat the experiment at home and find out what type of soil they had in their own gardens. This was the sort of homework the twins didn't mind – it was outside!

At home, Ailis and Aiden set about doing their homework. Their parents wondered what they were up to, digging in different corners of the garden. "It's homework. We're finding out what type of soil we have in our garden. It's an experiment," explained Aiden.

"We want to make sure we get a good mark, so we thought we would get on with it before the evening meal," Ailis informed Mum and Dad.

"We have to do the rest of the experiment inside, so may we have the cellar as our base?" Aiden asked. "That way, we can leave our stuff there and won't make a mess in our rooms," he added casually. Their parents agreed to the suggestion and, before they knew it, Ailis and Aiden were moving their stuff into the cellar to establish a base for their horticultural work. The cellar was gloomy, so Dad provided brighter light bulbs. He also gave them a brush, dustbin, some pots, a rug for the floor, an old table, a couple of chairs and even a comfy old settee – anything to get the twins interested in reading, writing and learning, thought Dad. When it was ready, the cellar looked like a great place for the two horticulturists to begin their work!

The twins followed the instructions that Mr Green had given them. When they rolled and squeezed their dried-out soil, they discovered that it just changed shape. "It's clay soil," they said, agreeing with each other.

"Let's write the results in our notebooks and then, after we've eaten, we can explore the cellar properly now that we have better light," suggested Ailis.

"Good idea," agreed Aiden, as they went to wash their hands before dinner. It was spaghetti bolognese – or 'spag bol' as they called it –their favourite!

After dinner, the twins returned to the cellar. They finished their homework and then started to look around carefully. It looked as if the cellar had once been divided into different rooms, and there were some small nooks at the back, far from the entrance and not easily seen in the shadows. They went into one of the nooks and were surprised to see a door. It was locked, but in the wall next to the door there was a small hole. Aiden, who did not mind spiders, put his hand into the hole and pulled out an old, rusty key. He tried it in the lock but, although it fitted, he could not turn the key. "We need to clean up the key and oil the lock," Ailis remarked. "Maybe we can do that at the weekend when we have more time."

As Allis and Aiden went back to their rooms to get ready to for bed, they wondered what they would find behind the door. This was turning into an adventure, thanks to Mr Green and his homework.

Chapter Four

On the way to school, the twins talked about the door they had found. "Do you think we should open it or leave it?" Ailis wondered.

"Open it of course. We may find treasure! Who knows?" Aiden was excited about the door and key.

At school, the horticulture lesson was interesting. Mr Green was pleased they had all done their homework and decided he would see who was really keen to work on the school garden; they would start preparing the area for planting. The class put on their gardening overalls and gloves and went out onto the field again. Each pair was given a spade and shown how to dig properly with it. Some squares had been marked out, and they were asked to dig in these and take out all the weeds. When the soil was weed-free, it could be hoed ready for planting.

The twins listened carefully to Mr Green and took their time. If you tried to dig too fast, you did not get the spade to the right depth in the soil and, if you did not take all the roots out, the weed would grow again. They progressed slowly, but soon their patch began to look clear of weeds and ready for hoeing. Mr Green said that those who were interested could continue to clear their area until the next lesson. He wanted to see who would keep going and who would leave; he would then be able to choose his gardening team.

The twins and a few of their classmates kept working all week, and they were delighted when they were chosen to be in the gardening team. The gardening team would do the real work in making the garden, while the rest of the class would learn how to plant seeds in pots and get them ready for the garden. The gardening team would have a couple of extra outdoor lessons each week, too, as long as they kept up with any work they missed in class. The twins' plan had worked – they had impressed Mr Green and were going to get more time out of class! They did not consider how hard they would have to work to keep up with their lessons and homework so that Mr Green would keep them on his team. They were too busy thinking about the door in the cellar. What was it for? Where did it lead? What would they find behind it?

On Saturday morning, Ailis and Aiden borrowed Dad's oil can, the one he used for his bike. They oiled the lock of the door in the cellar, cleaned the key carefully and then put some oil on that, too, so that it would turn more easily in the lock. "Now, we have to try it," said Aiden. Carefully, he put the key in the lock. He held his breath. Would it turn? There was a loud clunk as the latch slid back – the twins were delighted! Ailis picked up the torch she had brought and slowly pulled the door open. They were standing in front of a small space with another door in front of them and one more to the side. There was a key hanging beside each door – this was turning into a real mystery!

Just then they heard voices... They were coming from the other side of the door opposite them. They sounded like children's voices. The twins looked at each other and then Aiden banged on the door. There was silence! After a moment, a voice called, "Who's there?" It sounded like a girl's voice.

"It's Ailis and Aiden," Ailis called back. Aiden put the key beside the door into the lock and turned it. The door creaked open and a torch shone in their faces. "Hey," shouted Ailis. "The light is hurting our eyes!" As the light was lowered, they saw the faces of two children.

It turned out that the children who lived next door had been given the cellar under their house as a playroom. They all introduced themselves, and Ailis and Aiden learnt that the boy was called Steven, he was eight, and his sister was called Sarah, she had just turned ten. They all turned to look at the other door with the key hanging beside it.

"Shall we clean the lock up and try the key in it?" asked Steven.

"Yes, let's!" replied the others, but just then the twins heard their lunch bell. Their mum had rigged it up so that she wouldn't have to come down into the cellar every time she wanted them.

"We can come back after lunch and see what's behind it," Steven suggested.

"We should get a bell rigged up too; then we will know if we are wanted," said Sarah, who liked to be organised.

The children agreed to meet up after lunch to discuss opening the mystery door.

That afternoon, it was decided that Steven and Sarah would get their dad to put up a bell for them; they were sure that they could convince him it was a good idea. Sarah and Steven had also brought their two-way radios so the four children could talk to each other when the doors were closed. The twins thought this was a great idea – it would be useful and fun! Life was getting more exciting, all thanks to their interest in horticulture! It was agreed that they would all meet again the following Saturday to try the mystery door.

When they went to bed, Ailis and Aiden tried the two-way radios. It was fun saying, "Aiden calling. Are you there? Over," and getting a reply from Steven, who sounded a bit sleepy. Ailis and Sarah talked on their two-way radios and decided that they would bring some torches in case it was dark behind the unopened door. They all went to sleep that night wondering what they would discover behind the door in the cellar. Aiden imagined that there would be a secret passage. Ailis wondered if there would be treasure.

Sarah thought that they might find boxes of books – she was a keen reader – and Steven was certain it would just be a cupboard for storing things.

Chapter Five

The week dragged by, but Saturday morning finally arrived and the twins got up and hurried through their chores. They did their homework and took their horticulture books down to the cellar, which they were now calling their 'den'. First, they swept the floor and then they tidied up the soil research table and tried to make the den look interesting. They stuck up some pictures they had painted, put some cushions on the settee and brought down a bottle of water, a bottle of squash and some cups to make drinks. Of course, they added a packet of biscuits for sharing with their visitors. They felt their den was now a welcoming place. Their parents were pleased to see them working together and enjoying themselves.

After lunch, the twins explained to their parents that they would be busy in their den working, and they would see them for their evening meal, if that was OK. As Mum and Dad had work to do as well, they agreed to see them later. The evening meal would be at six o'clock. Ailis and Aiden were pleased; they would have plenty of time to find out if the mystery door would unlock and if it led anywhere.

The twins went down and cleaned and oiled the lock ready for trying the key. Aiden suddenly hushed Ailis,

"Listen, I think I hear knocking. It must be Steven and Sarah." They went to the door that divided the cellars and, using the two-way radios, made certain that Sarah and Steven were in their cellar and ready to come through. Aiden put the key in the door and unlocked it, and Sarah and Steven came through carrying a bag of supplies for their adventure. They had torches, four headbands with small torches attached to them and some cake. After they had said hello to each other and put the food supplies with the biscuits and drinks on the table, they were ready to try to open the mystery door.

Aiden took the key and put it in the keyhole. He paused, feeling a bit nervous. "Go on, try it," urged Steven. "Let's see if it works!"

"Right, here goes!" There was a creaking sound and slowly the key turned in the lock. Finally, there was a click. Aiden took a deep breath and carefully pushed open the door. The four children peered through.

"Torches on," instructed Sarah, and four torches were turned on and shone into the doorway.

"Wow," murmured Ailis, "it's not a cupboard or a treasure chest, is it?"

"No, it's a passage – a secret passage!" Aiden was happy, his dream had come true.

"We will have to go carefully. It will be dirty and we don't know how safe it is," Sarah sounded slightly worried. They shone the torches at the ceiling, the walls and the ground and saw that the tunnel was made of bricks. They were also able to breathe easily; rather than smelling stale and damp, the air seemed surprisingly fresh.

"I think it's safe to explore, as long as we move slowly and go one behind the other," Ailis wanted them all to stay safe. The boys agreed. Aiden said that he would go first, and Steven said he would bring up the rear. Aiden slowly began to move forward into the tunnel.

The tunnel was dark and Aiden shone his torch on the floor so he could see where he was walking. Their head torches showed spiders' webs hanging from the walls and ceiling. Luckily, none of them were bothered by spiders. They thought that some of the webs looked old, as if they had been spun a long, long time ago.

"I wondered who used this tunnel. It looks ancient – it must have some history, some stories to tell," Sarah whispered.

"I bet it has," replied Ailis, "but where is it taking us?"

"Maybe to hidden treasure," Steven smiled at that idea.

Suddenly, Aiden stopped. There were some steps in front of him that led downwards. The group of four stood thinking about what to do next. Ailis asked the question that they were all asking themselves, "Shall we go down them? We have plenty of time before we have to be back."

Sarah decided that she and Aiden would go down the steps to check they were safe. The other two could wait and go for help if it was needed. Steven and Ailis considered this idea and agreed. Aiden and Sarah decided they would follow the steps for 10 minutes and then return, so they set the alarms on their watches. Aiden walked down the first few steps shining his torch on them. He then turned round, using the light to help guide Sarah down to him. He did the same again and they found themselves in another tunnel. They walked along it until the 10-minute alarms sounded. Steven and Ailis were waiting at the top of the stairs. They were relieved to see the lights from Sarah and Aiden's torches as they made their way back.

When they were settled back in the den with their drinks and cake, Aiden and Sarah described what they had found. "The steps were very rough, and we had to be careful not to trip and fall," Sarah started their story.

"When we got to the bottom, the passage went on in front of us. It seemed to slope down for a while and then straightened out," continued Aiden, who was excited about their exploring and wanted to tell the others about it in detail. "As we walked along, we heard a rumbling above us that sounded like cars on a road. Then the passage started to climb upwards again, and we came to some more steps and – would you believe it? – another door!" He jumped up, laughing with excitement.

"We'll have to try the door, won't we?" questioned Steven.

"I wonder what's on the other side," Ailis wished she had been the explorer instead of Aiden.

Chapter Six

Sarah thought that they should have a break and check that they hadn't been missed by their parents. They needed to get to know each other properly, but they should visit each other using their front doors, too, so that their parents wouldn't get suspicious.

"I know, we can have a game of catch and 'accidentally' hit the ball into your garden. Then we can knock on your door to ask for it back!" Steven surprised them with his idea. It was easy, and they all decided it would work.

Steven and Sarah went back to their house and Aiden and Ailis tidied up the den. They went upstairs and found their parents having a cup of coffee in the kitchen.

"We were just coming to fetch you. We have finished our work and wondered if you would you like to go a walk along the front. It's a lovely day, and the exercise will do us all good," said Mum. The twins were wondering what to reply, when suddenly there was a thud in the garden. They all looked out of the window and saw a football lying on the grass.

"Oh dear," said Dad. "It looks like the children next door have kicked their ball into our garden. Well, not to worry, we can just throw it back."

"No!" the twins almost shouted.

"It would be nicer to give the ball back to them and get to know them," Ailis said.

Just then, there was a knock on the door. The twins raced to answer it. It was Sarah and Steven, grinning and looking quite pleased that they had managed to get the ball over the wall without breaking a window.

"Please may we have our ball back?" they asked laughing.

"Come in," invited the twins, smiling broadly. So far, so good! Ailis and Aiden introduced themselves and their parents. The children went into the garden to fetch the ball and they started kicking it around together. The twins' mum and dad told Sarah to invite her parents in for a coffee with them, and soon both families were chatting together and enjoying a walk along the seafront. The sea was calm and the swooshing of the waves on the shore was soothing. A ferry was going out towards France, and sail boats bobbed on the water. Children were running along the front, following the wavy pattern of the paving stones and trying not to bump into people.

The new friends were not able to do anymore exploring that day, but Steven and Sarah asked if they could meet up the next day, Sunday, to look at the horticultural project that the twins were working on. Their parents were a little surprised by the request but were happy to agree.

Sarah and Steven visited on Sunday afternoon as planned,

and they started to learn about the work Ailis and Aiden were doing at school. They both thought it sounded like fun, especially when they learnt that Ailis and Aiden got to miss lessons to work in the school garden. Maybe they could do something in their own garden. Sarah liked flowers, and a flower bed would be something interesting to look at through their windows.

"When are we going to explore the tunnel again and see if we can get through the door at the other end?" Aiden was keen to show the others what he and Sarah had found. He had been imagining what might be on the other side of the door.

"Let's have a quick explore now. We're not expected home until teatime," Sarah suggested. "Your parents are busy, so I think we have time."

They all agreed, gathered their keys and torches together and went through the secret door into the tunnel. They moved faster than before and were soon through the first part of the tunnel, down the steps, along the last part of the tunnel and in front of the door.

"Who's going to try a key?" asked Ailis.

"I hope one will fit. Let's try the one to our cellar," Sarah wanted to be first, but her key didn't work; neither did the one that Ailis tried. There was one left. Aiden gave it to Steven to try. Carefully, Steven put the key into the lock and slowly turned it. There was a clicking sound as the bolt slid back. They all looked at each other. It was difficult to believe their luck – the door was open!

Slowly, they pushed the door open. They were in a small opening to the side of an old building. There was an old iron fire escape above them and, looking through a gap in the boards in front of them, they saw what appeared to be a wild area – there were thick bushes, gangly weeds and small trees everywhere. Large pieces of wood – hoardings – hid the place from people passing by in the nearby street.

"Wow!" exclaimed Steven. "I wonder where we are."

Sarah pulled out her camera and took some photos. "Let's get back and see if there is any way we can work out where this place is. It's our own secret garden!" she was excited. She had seen a small fruit tree – things grew well here, she thought. Sarah was getting into horticulture; she had enjoyed reading about plants with the twins in their den.

Chapter Seven

When they got back to the house, the children went to Aiden and Ailis's dad to ask if he had any books and maps of old Southsea. They knew he was interested in history, and they thought he might have some pictures of what Southsea had been like in the past. This is a strange topic, the twins' dad thought. He wondered why they wanted the information. He found a couple of picture books of Southsea at the end of the war and left the children to look at them in the den. Sarah looked at the photo she had taken and the pictures in the book. "There are houses like ours in this street," she said. "It's near the Queen's Hotel, too. It could be our street."

"Do you think that the place we found is near the Queen's Hotel?" Steven was sure it was.

"It could be. If you look at this map, it shows our street and Osborne Road with the Queen's Hotel at the end of it. The passage could go under our street and come up near to it. After all, there are some hoardings behind the hotel," Aiden pointed out.

Ailis thought Aiden had solved the puzzle. Now they could get on with deciding what to do next. In the meantime, the twins had homework to do. At school, the gardening team had planted a few different plants in the garden. Mr Green had told them to research which other plants would grow well there, too.

Steven said, "It's a pity you can't just plant some to see which ones grow best."

"We can, can't we?" Aiden had an idea. "We could plant them on the land we just found to see what happens. If it's possible for an apple tree to grow there, why not other plants? It really will be our secret garden!"

They decided to give it a go.

The four children started to notice their neighbours' front gardens; some had tubs with plants in them, and some had planters that looked like little gardens. These seemed to attract insects that collected pollen and nectar. In one garden, they saw that the planter was empty. It belonged to an old lady who couldn't get about easily.

"I wonder if she would like some nice plants in her planter," Ailis was a kind girl, and she thought the old lady must miss seeing her planter filled with flowers. Aiden suggested putting some plants in her planter as a surprise. They had a few plants they could use, as Mr Green had allowed them to bring home some of the ones left over from the school garden. They were planting flowering plants at the moment, as they were still preparing the vegetable garden and had to plant potatoes first to help break up the soil.

Very early the next morning, before their parents were awake and while the street was still empty, the children met with their gardening tools. The sun was rising, the sky was blue and clear, and the street was peaceful. They quietly weeded the old lady's planter so the plants would have room to grow. Then they put the plants in and watered them. Sarah and Steven helped, so they finished the work quickly and then dashed home. If their parents were surprised that they were up before them, they decided not to question it – it made life easier than having to drag the children out of bed!

During the week, the children kept an eye on the planter and, one morning, they went out early to water the plants and dig out any new weeds. No one saw them and only the old lady had noticed the change in the planter. She thought it was strange that there were small plants growing there, and the weeds seemed to be disappearing...

"It's a mystery," she sighed. She felt lonely, but each day she looked out of her window and saw the planter. She felt happy that there were plants growing in her yard again and that someone seemed to care about her.

"We could put some of the spare plants in the secret garden," Aiden and Steven wanted to go back along the tunnels to their special place. The girls agreed. The next weekend when they were together in the den, they gathered together some plants, gardening tools and torches and set off along the passage. The noise of the road reminded them where they were. It seemed strange to be crossing a road by going under it!

The children looked out into the wild garden. Birds were singing in the branches of the trees, and some bushes had flowers blooming on them – the first blooms of spring.

"Look, there's a small clearing between those bushes. Let's put the plants in there," Aiden suggested. The children worked hard, pulling up weeds and digging over the soil. They put the plants in the ground, watered them from bottles of water they had carried in their packs and took a photo of them.

"It might be a while before we can come back, so let's hope these plants grow well," Sarah was certain this was a special place.

In the meantime, new plants had appeared in another tub in their street. The owner of the tub had injured his leg and had difficulty walking. When the children had noticed him struggling to tidy the tub up, they had decided to help – they enjoyed getting up before anyone else on the street to surprise their neighbours. The man looked out of his window and smiled when he saw the plants in his tub. He wondered who had planted them – magic perhaps!

Chapter Eight

At school, Ailis and Aiden learnt more about gardening. They learnt that you could make your own compost out of vegetable peelings, teabags, coffee granules, old flower heads and bits of newspaper. They had a large compost bin at school and had started a smaller one at home. Sarah and Steven also got their parents to recycle the garden and kitchen waste and had a compost bin in their garden.

They four children met up after school and, while they walked home, started looking out for places that would benefit from a plant or two. Their main problem was how to grow the plants they needed for their secret gardening work. As they were passing the tub they had planted, Aiden saw a weed and picked it out.

"Hey, you!" shouted an angry voice. "Leave my tub alone! Don't mess with my plants!"

Aiden said sorry and explained that it was a weed he had picked. The man just grunted.

"Wow!" declared Ailis. "He is fierce, isn't he?"

"I think he's just protecting his tub, as he's pleased it's got plants in it," said Sarah. Aiden felt a bit cross that he had been shouted at for picking a weed, but that was life. Steven wondered if the man was grumpy because he found it hard to do his gardening.

In the meantime, the man had phoned his friend Tim Green. Tim had a camera he wanted to borrow so that he could find out who was secretly looking after his tub. Tim thought it was a splendid idea. He came round, set up the camera and turned it on. "I'd like to see who you catch," he said to his friend, who was called Joe.

For the first few days, when they checked the footage, Tim and Joe saw nothing. Then, after a few days, the camera caught something early one morning – it was the children! They were tidying up the tub and adding another plant. Joe recognised them as the ones he had shouted at.

"I know two of them," said Tim. "They are in my gardening group. I expect the plants are ones I gave to them."

Joe wrote a note and Tim put it into the tub: *Please come and see me on Saturday morning at 10 o'clock.*

Early the next morning, the children found the note and decided they had better meet the man to explain what they were doing.

"Let's check our secret garden early that morning, before everyone is up. We've not checked how the plants are doing for a while," said Sarah.

"Then we can go and meet the man with the tub," Ailis

wondered if they were in trouble.

After meeting at five o'clock on Saturday morning, the four children made their way along the tunnels to the door that led to their secret garden. It was surprising how quickly the spiders could rebuild their webs, they thought. Aiden stepped into the garden cautiously, as they did not want to be caught there. They were not naughty children, but they were not sure who the wild area belonged to.

"All clear," Aiden spoke quietly, because the birds were singing and he did not want to scare them. The others came through the door and they all made their way to the clearing.

"Wow!" gasped Steven. "Look at that!" The plants had not died; they had grown, and the children were surprised to see how lovely they looked. The plants had seemed tiny and fragile when they planted them; now, they looked healthy and lush.

"We can use this land to plant small plants and then, when they are ready, we can put them into the planters and tubs of people who need our gardening help," said Sarah. She was excited to see how well the plants had grown.

"We can take photos and see which ones grow best," Ailis wanted their experiment to go well.

"We'll have to make some plant pots, as we can't buy them," declared Aiden. He thought it was important not to waste materials when you were gardening. Mr Green has said that you should use plant pots that you could recycle in some way.

When they had weeded and cleared some more ground for planting, the children returned to their homes so that they could go back to bed for a while. They would meet up again later.

"We mustn't forget our ten o'clock meeting," said Steven.

"I wonder what he wants," Aiden was worried the grumpy man might want to speak to their parents and they would get in trouble.

At exactly ten o'clock, the four children were stood in front of the grumpy man's door. Aiden took a deep breath and knocked. They heard footsteps in the hallway and then the door swung open. Ailis and Aiden gasped – it was Mr Green!

"I was interested to see who my friend Joe's secret gardeners were," he told the children. "I couldn't believe my eyes when I saw you two on the film."

The children explained to Mr Green and Joe what they had been doing in their neighbours' gardens. The two men heard how the children had spotted the old lady's planter and Joe's tub and thought that they might like some plants in them.

"I like seeing the plants growing in my tub," said Joe. "It was a kind thing to do. But you must be certain, if you do such a thing again, that you don't damage any plants already growing," he added.

"We have decided to become Southsea's secret gardeners," the children told Joe.

"Hmm, I'll have to think about what to do," said Mr Green. The foursome hoped he wouldn't tell their parents straight away.

"We thought we could put plants and seeds in areas where there aren't any," blurted Steven.

"That's an idea – to use wasted spaces and put plants in them. I have heard of groups doing that in some other towns," said Mr Green. "Maybe we can look into that and do something special for a wasteland area. Certainly, it could be done with help of the school gardeners," he added.

Chapter Nine

The children promised to keep looking after Joe's tub until he could get about again. Joe didn't mind when they did the work, so they decided to keep doing it in the early mornings for a while longer – they liked the idea of being secret gardeners! In the meantime, they put a circle of different plants in their hidden garden and waited to see how they would grow. They didn't know that a member of staff at the hotel had seen the plants. She was certain they had been planted and wondered if someone who worked at the hotel had put them there. However, when asked, none of the other staff knew anything about the plants in what they thought of as the wild area. The staff member, whose name was Amanda, considered what to do next. She was kept very busy with her work, but would keep an eye out for the secret gardeners.

Later that day, Amanda was out jogging when she ran into a friend. Over coffee, she told him about her find behind the hotel.

"I bet I know who your secret gardeners are," her friend told her. It was Mr Green!

"How could you know who they are?" asked Amanda

"Well, my friend Joe has had some secret gardeners taking care of his tub. We put up a camera to catch them on film, and two of them were members of my gardening group!" Mr Green laughed. "They certainly seem to be getting about!"

"But Tim, how are they getting into the wild area? I can only get to it from the hotel," questioned Amanda. Tim and Amanda did not have an answer to that question – it was a bit of a mystery.

"We will put up a camera and make certain that it is them," said Mr Green. "I will have a serious talk with them, if it is."

Once again, Mr Green put up his camera and set it to record. After checking the camera each day, they saw four figures appear early on Saturday morning, carrying gardening tools. They watched as they tidied up the planted area and then left. Mr Green thought it looked like Sarah, Steven, Ailis and Aiden.

"How did they get in?" asked Amanda. "I didn't see."

"I didn't notice either," said Mr Green. "We need to have a chat with them. Let's wait here early next Saturday, as they seem to visit at the weekend."

"OK, but we'll have to get up early to catch them," sighed Amanda.

In the meantime, Ailis, Aiden, Sarah and Steven had been discussing what to do. "We should tell our parents before Mr Green does," Aiden supposed their parents would find out what they had been up to one way or another.

"Or, we could wait and see what Mr Green says," Ailis chipped in. She was enjoying going out in the morning and tending to Joe's tub and the old lady's planter.

Sarah thought they should check on the garden behind the hotel. "At least that is still secret," she said.

The children decided they would go and check the garden early next Saturday, before seeing to the areas of their own gardens that they had been allowed to grow plants in. They had started working together and, that way, more gardening work got done. Their parents talked together about how pleased they were that their children were friends and so keen on gardening.

"The twins' marks at school are really good now. I think it's all the extra reading and research they have been doing," their dad said.

"They have been sending emails to their grandparents to get advice, as well," said their mum.

"Sarah and Steven really enjoy working together on the garden," said their mum. "It's a good thing your twins started having lessons in horticulture at their school."

Little did they know about the secret gardening – that was a surprise still to come!

On Saturday, the children met in the den as usual and

gathered together all the things they might need. They wanted to bring back a couple of plants for Joe's tub to make it more colourful. Aiden led the way but as he pushed open the door to the garden, he paused – he heard voices.

"Turn off the torches," he hissed. "Someone's out there!"

Aiden pulled the door back so that it was nearly closed, and they all listened.

"I wonder when they'll appear, Tim," said an unknown voice.

"It's still early. Perhaps they have slept in this morning. I really want to see where they get into the garden," replied a male voice that they had heard before – it was Mr Green!

Aiden reached an arm round the door and gently pulled some ivy in front of it. He locked the door quietly and they all returned to the den.

"The lady who spoke must be from the hotel, and Mr Green must know her," Sarah had guessed that Mr Green knew who he was waiting for.

"Well, they haven't found the door, and I covered it with hanging ivy before I closed it," reported Aiden.

"But Mr Green must know it's us if he was there," moaned Ailis.

"What next?" demanded Steven.

The four talked about what they could do. Should

they tell their parents about the passage and their secret gardening, or should they wait to see what happened next? What did happen next was a big surprise!

Chapter Ten

The twins were in their horticulture lesson, when Mr Green told the class that Ailis and Aiden had given him an idea, and the owner of the Queen's Hotel had agreed that they could visit to see if they could develop a garden there. The gardening group were very excited. As they got their coats and tools and piled onto the school bus, Aiden and Ailis tried to breathe calmly – they had not expected a trip to the Queen's Hotel!

Amanda was waiting for the school gardeners at the entrance to the hotel. The owner, Mr Farid, who had given permission for the gardening project, was with her. He welcomed the children and told them a little about the hotel's history. There had been a hotel on the site since 1865, but the original hotel had burnt down and been rebuilt. He was now restoring the building so that guests and local people could see what a beautiful place it was. The children were impressed; the hotel had a really grand look about it. Mr Farid hoped they would enjoy their gardening project.

Amanda took Mr Green and the children through a gate and suddenly they were in a wild garden – the twins' secret garden! Ailis and Aiden felt sad that their special garden was no longer a secret but a school project. The others in the group were really excited; they were going to make a proper garden area for the hotel! It would have wild flowers, herbs and flowering plants. It would be designed to attract bees, butterflies and other small creatures that liked to live in sheltered spaces. As the other children congratulated the twins on their amazing idea, Ailis and Aiden began to see that everyone in the group would enjoy this work. They were pleased, but what would they tell Sarah and Steven?

Once everyone had started work, Mr Green took Ailis and Aiden to one side. He looked serious. The twins wondered what was coming.

"Now you two, how on earth did you get into this place and start a garden in it?" he demanded in a quiet but firm voice. The twins had to think quickly – they wanted to tell their parents and Sarah and Steven first.

"We think it would be a good idea if you visited us on Saturday morning, so our parents can meet you first," Ailis was serious too. She wanted their parents to be with them and to know what they had been up to so there were no surprises.

"OK, until Saturday then. Now, go and get on with your work. You have done a good job on the planting, by the way." Praise indeed from Mr Green!

That night Southsea's secret gardeners had an urgent meeting.

"I think we should tell our parents and show them the passage before Saturday," said Ailis. "They can decide if we should tell Mr Green about it."

"It must have some link to the Queen's Hotel. The hotel is very old and has been there a long time." Sarah, who liked history, had heard the hotel's story from the twins.

That night both families got together, and the children told their parents what had been going on.

"We just wanted to be secret gardeners and to give the old lady and Joe some joy," Steven told the adults.

"Well, you were being kind, but you really should have told us," their parents told them, lots of times.

"It's the passage you found that I'm curious about," said the twins' dad. "You need to show it to us, and we can check that it is safe." He was keen to see the secret passage – he wished he had found it.

Chapter Eleven

Early the next morning, the two families met in the cellar at the entrance to the passage.

"Wow, to think this has been here and not been found before seems very strange!" The twins' dad had a camera and was busy taking photos. He wanted to have a record of the passageway. The children led the way, telling their parents to watch their heads. Surprisingly, the passage was high enough for them to walk along it without banging their heads. Their parents had good torches and their beams picked out initials on the bricks and names with dates.

"I wonder who they were," Sarah was filled with curiosity.

"Perhaps they were the people who built the passageway," said her mother. "People often like to let you know they have had something to do with a building." She too was curious about the names. She had noticed that the dates were around the time the hotel would have been built. Was there a link between the hotel and the house they lived in?

When they reached the door, Aiden unlocked it. They spilled into the now not-so-secret garden only to find themselves face to face with the owner of the hotel. He had come down before his breakfast to look at the work the children had done.

"Why, hello! Where did you come from?" Mr Farid remembered the children from the school group and wondered what they were doing.

"We're the secret gardeners," Ailis told him. "We found a passage that leads from our house to here, and we began to make a garden. I'm sorry if we did wrong," she added.

"Well, we now have a great project going with your school, so good has come out of it," replied Mr Farid. "Come and join me for a special Queen's Hotel breakfast," he added.

The families had a lovely breakfast and the four children told Mr Farid all about their gardening activities. "All to get out of the classroom?" Mr Farid laughed. "I bet you are doing more schoolwork now than ever!"

"They're certainly getting good marks for their work," laughed the twins' mum.

After their breakfast, which they really enjoyed, the two families took Mr Farid to the hidden door. Pushing back the ivy, Aiden led them all through the door and along the passage to the cellar of their house. They ended up in the kitchen, around the table, talking about the passage and who may have built it.

"I'll have to see if there is anything in the hotel records," Mr Farid said. He was looking forward to seeing if these houses were connected to the hotel in some way.

Just then the doorbell rang. The twins looked at each other in horror – Mr Green! In all the excitement, they had forgotten to tell their parents that he was going to call.

Mr Green was invited into the kitchen. He was surprised to see the other two children, their parents and Mr Farid. He explained why he had called and said that he was glad to see the children had told their parents about their gardening adventures.

"I was concerned about how they were getting into the garden," he told the parents.

"You need to come with us," said Sarah's dad.

Soon they were all back in the hotel garden. Mr Green could hardly believe that they had found a secret passage that led them to the place.

"I can see why you liked it – it is a lovely space for growing things and listening to the birds," he said. "I bet you were sad when we found you out, but now all the children in the gardening group have a special place, too."

"Indeed they do, and the children have my permission to use the passage to come here anytime, providing they let their parents know." Mr Farid addressed the group. "I will tell my staff to look out for them. Now, I must get back to the hotel, and I will let you know if I find anything in the records."

Chapter Twelve

The children had a new plant for the old lady's planter, and it was decided that it was time for her to meet her secret gardeners. Steven knocked on her door and, when she answered, they told her their story.

"I was so pleased that someone cared enough to look after my planter," said the old lady, who introduced herself as Mary Brown. "I hurt my ankle and it has taken a while to get better. I have been lonely, as I couldn't get out and about. I've enjoyed looking out of my window and seeing the plants grow. Please will you keep looking after them, at least until I can get about more easily?"

The children were relieved that Mary Brown liked what they had done and promised to look after her planter. They also decided to call on her when they could – they did not like to hear that she was lonely.

Mr Farid found out that the houses where the two families lived had been built for the hotel and some of the staff had lived in them. They had used the passage to travel to and from the hotel safely and easily without having to go outside. Some of the names on the passage walls matched names on old staff records, and others were those of people who had built the passageway.

Once friends and neighbours learnt about Southsea's secret gardeners, they began to ask the children to look after their tubs and planters, too. The hotel now had a lovely new garden for the guests to enjoy and the school garden had been a great success, so Mr Green was able to start new projects for the children, helping others who wanted to see their gardens or unused spaces flourish. All of the children in the gardening group helped, and Mr Green kept a close eye on them.

Ailis, Aiden, Sarah and Steve decided that getting interested in horticulture had turned out to be the best idea ever! Maybe they would be professional gardeners when they were older but, for the time being, they were just enjoying helping Southsea to bloom.

READ ON FOR THE
NEXT BOOK IN THE SERIES

KEEPING up WITH
the Greens

SHELAGH MOORE

●

A SAMPLE CHAPTER

CHAPTER ONE
"I want a loo roll!"

"Aaargh!!!" There was a loud – very loud – yell from the bathroom. It was Fred. Fred did not do things quietly; in fact, Fred had a loud voice and was a very noisy boy. The Green family found him hard work at times. However, under all the noise, he had a kind heart. Fred had gone to the loo, but disaster had struck – when he reached out to take some toilet paper, it was gone! Hence the loud – very loud – yell. All that was left was the cardboard roll that the toilet paper should have been wrapped around.

Fred knew his mum had been shopping and he hoped she had bought some loo rolls.

"Sorry Fred, there were no loo rolls in the shops today. People have been buying them and there were none left," she explained. "I did think we still had a couple left."

Fred groaned. What on earth was he going to do? He soon found out. "You'll have to use the baby wipes" his mum told him. "Put them in the bin by the toilet as they can't be flushed."

Fred was furious. "I'm not a baby!" he yelled, waking the baby. "I'm not in nappies – I want a loo roll!"

Fred's mum threw the baby wipes in to him and left

him to it while she went to soothe the baby, who was now wide awake and wanted feeding. She sighed. It's a pity Fred could not do things more quietly like his brother Joe and sister Josephine, she thought. They were doing their schoolwork and keeping very quiet. But Joe and Josephine were waiting to see what Fred would do next – they, too, were not keen on baby wipes!

After some time Fred came out of the bathroom looking cross. He had used the baby wipes, put them in the bin and washed his hands carefully while singing 'Happy Birthday' twice to himself, as they had learnt to do in school. He missed school – not the work, but his friends. He enjoyed playing football with them at break time. In the classroom, he tried his best, but he did prefer the lessons like PE, drama and art where you could express yourself more. His brother and sister enjoyed school, as they liked learning about new things. They were older than Fred who was seven; Joe was nine and Josephine was nearly eleven and ready for secondary school. She felt quite grown up. Joe enjoyed playing jokes on people, but he did tend to forget what he was doing if he got distracted and became interested in something else.

"When will you be shopping again, Mum?" asked Fred.

"Not for a while," replied his mum. "I did a really big shop as it's such a trek into town." They lived on the edge of a village in Yorkshire. "We will have to make do with baby wipes until I go shopping again. We've got plenty of them. Now, go and play with your football. I'll call you in when lunch is ready."

Fred went out into the garden. He was not in the mood for football. He wandered round the garden, which was big and had a pond, a climbing frame and a vegetable garden in it. He kicked some leaves about, watched a frog sitting on a lily pad on the pond for a while and then went to find his brother and sister. They looked at him and wondered what he wanted.

"Have you any loo rolls hidden away?" he asked suspiciously; they did play tricks on him sometimes.

"No, we have not," said Josephine. "We have to use baby wipes too, you know."

"Why don't we find out what happened when people didn't have loo rolls?" Joe said. They agreed; it might be helpful to know what could be used instead of baby wipes.

Mum was pleased to see the children doing something together and not bickering. She was tired; the shopping had taken a long time and putting everything away after she had settled the baby for a nap left her feeling like having a nap herself. She sat by the baby, who was sleeping peacefully in her small cot downstairs, closed her eyes and dozed. She hadn't heard what the children planned to do, but she would find out soon.

Josephine used the internet on her computer and Joe looked at one of their books on history. They had a lot of books in their house, and they all enjoyed reading and finding out about things. They found out a lot of facts about what people did before toilet paper was invented. Early man used moss and leaves when they went to the toilet! "Do you think we could do that?" asked Fred. "I wonder if there are any leaves that might do for us." They hunted around the garden. There was a lot of moss around the trees, and some bushes had quite large leaves. Josephine didn't think she would like to use moss in case there were any creepy crawlies hiding in it. Joe thought there was a risk that if you used the wrong sort of leaves, such as giant hogweed, you could get a rash or feel poorly. Fred wasn't sure; he thought the moss would be soft, but agreed that there probably was not enough and getting rid of it would be tricky, as they could not flush it away. They also knew that there was no way their mum would allow them to bring it into the house for use in the bathroom, but it was useful to know about moss and leaves if they ever went camping

Next, they looked at what the Romans did. They knew about the Romans and thought they were good at this sort of thing, as they had toilets in their houses. Romans used something called a spongia or tersorium. A spongia was a sea sponge on a stick that they used to clean themselves. It was kept in salt water or seawater between uses.

"We've not got any sea sponges, so that won't work," said Joe.

"I don't know about that. We've got our own sponges,

and we could fix them to hazel sticks. We could each have our own spongia in a bottle of salt water," said Fred, who was keen to try this instead of the baby wipes.

They thought about the idea and decided to give it a go. They each chose a hazel stick and carefully cut their sponges so that they fitted onto the sticks. They were all ready to use their new wipers instead of having to use baby wipes.

It was not until Mum went into the bathroom and found three bottles of saltwater holding sponges on sticks that their plan began to unravel.

"What are these?" she asked in a shrill voice. She actually knew what they were, as she was a teacher – she knew more about them than the children did.

"We thought we would try them instead of baby wipes, which we don't like using 'cos we're not babies," Josephine spoke loudly and firmly to her mum.

"I don't think so. I know what these are, and I also know they are not as clean or safe as baby wipes. They are not to be used," Mum replied, as she picked up the bottles and took them out of the bathroom. "Use the baby wipes," her voice faded as she went downstairs to dispose of the homemade spongias.

"Well that worked well... Not!" said Joe and Fred almost together.

"What else is there to try?" Joe added.

The three children went back to their research. That night, on WhatsApp with their dad, Mum sounded amused. "Can you imagine it? They did research and found out about things that can be used instead of loo rolls, because they don't want to use baby wipes!" Their dad, who was in the army and working away from home, had a good laugh, "I bet they won't give up. You'd better be on the lookout for what's next!" He was smiling at the thought of his children trying to get out of using baby wipes. At least they were working together, he thought. It was a good story to tell his fellow soldiers, who knew all too well what it was like to be out in the wilds on a training exercise without loo rolls!

Next, the children looked at what other countries did before loo roll was invented. They found that the Chinese had invented a type of toilet paper. It was made from mulberry bark, hemp and rags mixed with water, which were bashed into a pulp and then pressed until all the water came out. "Mmm, we could do that," Joe said. They could make the 'paper' in the garden and then bring it into the house for their own personal use. They went into the garden and dragged out a small metal bathtub that was used to hold the washing when Mum was pegging it out on the line. They went round the garden looking for some bark. There was some hemp that Mum had been using to make sacks for garden waste, and they found some old cloth, which they could cut up, at the back of the garden shed.

Mum was watching the children out of the kitchen window.

"I wonder what they are up to now?" she said to herself.

It reminded her of a story about their dad when he was about five. He loved making 'potions'. He would get a bowl and put twigs, grass, berries and all sorts into it, and then he would stir it well. His potions always looked disgusting and were usually poured out in a corner of the garden! She was just about to go into the garden and ask them what they were doing when the baby woke up. She would have to find out what they were up to later!

Fred, Joe and Josephine mixed everything together. They then got their cricket and rounders bats and started to mash the mix to a pulp. When they had finished doing that, they got some flagstones and put them on top of the pulp. The water slowly ran out through the plug hole at the bottom of the tin bath.

"We've got to get it as dry as we can," panted Joe. "The pulp has to be pressed dry so that it makes paper."

By the time they had finished, there was a big pile of flagstones pressing down on the pulp mix.

The children went in for their tea and then played with their baby sister. That night they watched a film and went to bed when they were told. They were tired – it had been a busy day. Later that night, Mum was talking to their dad. "They were up to something in the garden today. It tired them out. Would you believe they went to bed without any fuss?" She sighed, "Sometimes I do wonder how much they are missing school and their friends." Dad told her not to worry – they seemed happy enough when they chatted to him. He was hoping to talk to them in a few days when he was off duty. He was part of a team of soldiers that was helping doctors and carers to deal with an outbreak of a virus in the UK. He told his wife not to worry, just to keep the children at home and stay safe and well until he saw them.

After a couple of days, the children, led by Joe, went to the tin bath. They took off the flagstones, piled them back in the corner by the garden shed and then looked at the pulp. It was almost dry! They got a large basket and carefully lifted the pulp sheet into it. They walked to the far end of the washing line and hung the sheet on the line to dry in the hot sun. They felt quite pleased with themselves – homemade toilet paper at last! Later in the day, they went out with a small basket each and carefully cut the sheet into squares before sharing them between them.

"We will have to put them in a bucket after we've used them. Then we can take them out to the compost heap at the end of the garden," said Josephine.

"I hope they work. I'm fed up of baby wipes!" said Fred in his loud voice.

When Mum went into the bathroom that evening, she saw the baskets and thought, "What now?" She called the children into the bathroom. "Explain please," she demanded, with her arms folded and a stern look on her face. Joe told her about their research into toilet paper substitutes.

"We thought it was a good idea," he told her hopefully. Their mum thought for a while.

"OK, you can try them for two days and then report back to me on how you are doing."

The children were delighted, but their delight did not last long. The homemade toilet paper broke up in their hands and was rough and unpleasant to use. After two days, they decided they would use the baby wipes after all, as they were much more comfortable. Mum was smiling when she talked to Dad and told him what they had been doing. He thought it was quite funny! "I'll send them a present," he said. "I think they will be pleased when they get it."

A few days later, a big parcel arrived for the family. Inside was a box for each of them, and in each box there was a pair of slippers and a loo roll! Even Mum got a loo roll, as well as a lovely scarf. The baby was happy with the rattle Dad had sent her. "Loo rolls – the best present ever!" the children said to each other. Their mum was just pleased that their experiments had finally come to an end.